Delicious Orcish Recipes by Grûsh the Disgusting

By Nicolas Lavertu

Greetings, human! I, Grûsh the Disgusting, want to introduce you to orcish culinary art. I am an excellent cook and have discovered plenty of extraordinary recipes. Not many orcs have died tasting them... well, not too many, anyway!

In this book, I will show you my best recipes so that you can become as strong and courageous as an orc. You need to eat like an orc to become strong like an orc. I hope you enjoy them and share them with your friends so that my art can be recognized among other peoples. Bon appétit!

LIST OF RECIPES

STICKY BREAKFAST

As an orc, I have a super delicious breakfast recipe to start the day like a warrior chef! You'll need eggs, bread, larvae, sauce, mushrooms, and lichen.

First, take the bread, slice it, and toast it over high heat. While doing that, crack the eggs into a bowl. Mix the eggs with larvae to provide protein for muscles and endurance.

Take the mushrooms and lichen, cut them into small pieces, and mix them with the eggs and larvae. Add a pinch of salt to enhance the flavor.

When the bread is toasted, place the egg-larvae-mushroom-lichen mixture on the bread. But you're not done yet! Take the strange sauce that you find in the woods and pour it over the egg-larvae-mushroom-lichen-bread mixture.

Now, eat up and feel super strong to fight enemies. I guarantee you'll win the battle with this in your belly!

SORCERER'S BRAIN

I have a recipe to become intelligent like a sorcerer! You'll need a sorcerer's brain, vegetable juice, a sorcerer's staff, fire, and your hands.

First, you need to find a sorcerer and squash their head to take their brain. The brain is the best thing for intelligence, everyone knows that! Put the brain in a bowl.

Now, you need vegetable juice. Even though it's disgusting, it seems to make you smart. So, pour the vegetable juice over the brain in the bowl.

But you're not done yet! Take the sorcerer's staff and break it into small pieces. Put the staff pieces on the brain in the bowl. Now, you need fire to cook the brain. Light a fire and place the bowl over it.

When the brain is cooked, eat it with your hands. Hands are the best for tasting food! You'll feel intelligence coming into your head. Now, you'll be smarter than all the other orcs!

Note: Eating a sorcerer's brain can drive you mad.
But don't be afraid, you're a strong and intelligent orc now!

GRUB GRATIN

I have a super delicious recipe for breakfast! You'll need grubs, a grub nest, a large bowl, melted cheese, and your fists to punch.

First, you need to find a grub nest, any kind will do. Grubs taste great in the mouth, especially when they're wriggling. Everyone knows that! Take the live grubs and put them in a large bowl.

Now, pour melted cheese over the grubs in the bowl. But you're not done yet! Give a gentle punch to the cheese to make the grubs angry. Angry grubs taste better! Roll the grubs in the cheese to coat them well.

Now, eat quickly before the grubs die. Dead grubs don't taste good, everyone knows that! Eat with your hands to feel the movement of the grubs in your mouth.

Note: Eating grubs can give you a stomach ache. But don't be afraid, you're a strong and brave orc! And now you have a super delicious breakfast to start the day like a warrior chef!

ELF SAUSAGES

I don't like elves. Elves are too beautiful and smell good, which disgusts me. But I really enjoy eating elf sausages, they are incredibly delicious. You need to find an elf and beat them to death. It's easy for me because I'm very strong. Then you will cut the elf's hair and keep it for decoration. It will look nice.

Turn the entire elf into sausages without any waste. To do that, you will use pig intestines. They are perfect for making sausages. Place the elf's beautiful hair on top of the sausages, it will be very impressive.

When I invite my friends to eat, I serve them elf sausages to impress them. The ladies especially love this dish. I recommend making a lot of sausages because they are not very filling, so you will eat a lot.

BLOOD PUDDING

I have a delicious recipe for you! First, you go to dungeons or human villages and punch people in the nose to make them bleed a lot. Collect all the blood in a big cauldron and add bark flour and bone powder. Then, you need a gelatinous monster to hold everything together. You can find one in the dark forest where the trees have eyes. The gelatinous monster is slimy and sticky, but don't be afraid, you are a strong orc!

Mix everything together in the cauldron, stirring vigorously as if it were the head of a villain. Be careful not to burn yourself with the hot blood, it hurts a lot. The mixture should be thick and sticky; otherwise, it won't be good.

When everything is well mixed, take the cauldron and empty its contents onto a plate. It may not look pretty, but that's what makes it delicious!

DWARF COTTON CANDY

I don't like dwarves. Dwarves are mean to me and my friends, always trying to steal our caves to take precious gems. Dwarves may be small but strong, excellent warriors, but I am better. I always win against dwarves; I am stronger.

I am clever and have invented a recipe to humiliate dwarves. I call it dwarf cotton candy. The recipe is easy, let me explain. First, cut the beards of the defeated dwarves and make a big ball out of the beards. I put it on the end of a wooden stick and sprinkle lots of rainbow-colored powder on top.

For dwarves, their beards are very precious, and they get very angry when they see us eating their colorful beards. But me and my friends, we enjoy eating their beards. We often eat their beards before a big battle against them, it's amusing. Dwarves get so upset when they see us eating their beards.

WYVERN EYE STEW

I may not be very clever, but I know how to make a disgustingly good meal. This dish is quite challenging to prepare as it's not easy to find wyverns; they fly too high. If you're lucky, you can kill one by throwing a big rock with force. Search in the swamp waters to find random mushrooms. I don't know if the mushrooms are good or not, but I add them anyway.

I take a cauldron and put the meat and mushrooms inside. No need to cut the meat into small pieces; I leave it large. I fill the cauldron with swamp water. I light a fire and let the meat and mushrooms boil. It's better to stir vigorously to mix everything.

Next, I add goblin eyes to give it a crunchy texture. I'm not sure if goblin eyes are good or not, but I think they add flavor. Stir even harder to mix everything well.

I wait for a little while, not too long because I'm hungry. When the meat and mushrooms are boiled and the goblin eyes are well mixed, I serve a big lump of stew.

GIANT RAT SOUP

I am hungry. I search for food in the caves and find many rats everywhere. The rats have long, hairy tails, and I understand that they are good to eat. I take a big stick and knock out the rats and put them in a big cauldron.

I gather larva juice, eggs, mushrooms, and onions. I put everything in the cauldron with the rats. I stir it with a big stick, or else the rats will stick to the bottom and not cook properly. I let it cook for a while until everything is hot and the smell becomes strong.

I take a bowl and fill it with the rat soup. I feel proud; I have managed to make a delicious meal with what I found in the caves. I eat the soup, making loud "slurp slurp" sounds to show that I am content.

I recommend giant rat soup to all orcs who are looking for an easy-to-make meal. Eat it every day to stay strong and healthy.

HELL'S HOT CHOCOLATE

One day, a wizard came into my cave. I wasn't pleased, so I smashed his head with a big axe. The wizard had a small magic wand. I was curious, so I took the magic wand and accidentally stirred it in a cup of hot chocolate.

Suddenly, a red, smoky magical portal appeared in the cup. I didn't understand how it worked. I asked the great shaman for an explanation. He told me that swirling the magic wand in the cup created a magical portal to the 8th Hell's Fountain of Naxiraxipharaelle, the Archdevil of Primordial Darkness.

I found it very interesting and decided to drink this warm and delicious liquid. It gave me great strength and fury. Perfect before going into battle to become invincible.

I became wary. Sometimes demons try to pass through the portal. I'm always vigilant, striking the little heads that occasionally poke out. I won't let the demons take my magical cup of hot chocolate. I'll remain the only one with the cup of magic.

BORBOG SANDWICH

I crave borbogs. Finding borbogs is easy. I go for a swim in the foul-smelling old marsh. It stinks, but I'm not afraid. I dive into the black, slimy water. I emerge with wrinkled skin and a body covered in stuck borbogs.

Now, I have borbogs. But how do I eat them? I tear off all the borbogs and cook them in carcass gelatin. The gelatin tastes good and gives me strength. No need for salt or pepper. Just gelatin and borbogs. Yum yum!

Next, I take very stale bread slices. The bread is hard as a rock. But I am strong and can bite into it. I put the borbogs inside. The borbogs are juicy, like fruits. I bite into them and feel the juices flowing in my mouth.

The meal is ready. The orc is happy. I eat the borbogs and dry bread and drink the carcass gelatin. It's delicious to me, but maybe not to humans. Humans are weak, they don't understand the taste of borbogs and gelatin but I am an orc, I know how to appreciate it.

MIXED GRILL BBQ

I love to eat. Sometimes, while wandering through dungeons, I go on a rampage, killing everything that moves. But I don't leave the corpses lying around. I bring them back to the cave to have a big BBQ.

First, I light a wood fire and place a grill over it. Now, I take all the bodies and put them on the grill. Mmmh, it already smells good!

I wait a little, smelling the scent of burning. It's time to flip the bodies to cook them well on both sides. Meanwhile, I prepare a special marinade to add a surprising flavor.

I mix dragon blood, ogre bile, and troll sweat. It gives a strong and spicy taste. I brush the marinade onto the bodies while they cook. Now, the aroma becomes even stronger and more delicious!

Finally, the bodies are well-cooked and nicely browned. I take them off the grill and place them on a large platter. Everyone takes one and eats until they are no longer hungry. It's a good meal full of surprising flavors.

PHOENIX CHICKEN

I enjoy eating phoenix meat. Phoenix meat is incredibly delicious but very challenging to cook. The phoenix is a not-so-friendly bird. When I kill it, it bursts into flames and comes back to life. It's mean, pecking and scorching the skin.

I have found a trick to eat phoenix. I take a large plate and fill it with earthworms, then I place the phoenix on top. The phoenix loves to eat earthworms, so I give it a mighty blow with a hammer. It dies, and I have a few seconds to start eating the phoenix meat.

But when the phoenix resurrects in a fiery explosion, I quickly deliver another blow with the hammer. I continue doing this until I am no longer hungry. It's important to let the bird go when I'm done, or it will set everything on fire!

GATOW

I enjoy eating gatow. I want to make gatow like humans do. To make gatow, I steal human ingredients. They call it sugar, but I don't know where it comes from.

I take bark flour and lizard eggs. I also add troll-butterfly larvae extract. I mix everything vigorously. I put it all in a large bowl and place it over a fire.

I wait. The fire is hot, and I feel the warmth. I sense the gatow cooking. I don't know for how long. Maybe a long time. Maybe not long. I don't know.

I look at the gatow. It doesn't look good. I decorate the gatow with insects found under rocks. The insects look delicious. Now, I eat the gatow. The gatow looks disgusting, but I enjoy it.

MARSH SUSHI

I had an epic battle with a wizard. He teleported us to a faraway land. They ate strange food there with peculiar plants they call rice. It also includes seaweed and fish. I took a small piece to bring back here and to let you taste.

But alas, there is no rice here! So, I had an idea: I took many ant eggs, which resemble rice a lot. But to make it stick together, I added troll mucus. It gives it a sticky texture, but it's good for the taste.

Next, I plunged my hands into the marsh to catch strange creatures. After that, I chopped them into small pieces and placed them on the ant eggs. But something was missing... Ah yes! I rolled it in marsh hay to add an earthy and crunchy taste.

And now, the meal is ready! But there's no need to heat it up, as we'll eat it cold like the animals. So, are you ready to try it?

HEALING SOUP

I know how to make a healing soup to help you recover if you're sick or injured. Listen carefully, you need to find creatures that move swiftly to make the soup. I recommend birds, rabbits, cats, snakes, and eels. Catch as many as you can and put them in a large pot of boiling water. Be careful of their sharp teeth and claws.

Next, add forest leaves. I don't know the names of the leaves, but you should look for ones that look good. Maybe brightly colored leaves work well in the soup. Then, add spiky fruits to aid in healing. The fruits with thorns are the best, they may hurt but are good for you.

Lastly, add pink mushrooms. They make you sleep, but they are good for you. You need sleep to heal. Add plenty of pink mushrooms to the soup, and you'll sleep like a baby.

ELEMENTAL GATOW

One day, I attacked a wizard tower. He was busy brewing a magical potion, so I quickly fought him and stole many strange bottles for my kitchen.

I was very curious, so I tried all the bottles to make gatow. Suddenly, the gatow caught fire! Then it was struck by lightning! Then water spilled all over the plate! I was scared, but my appetite was stronger than my fear so I tried to eat a piece of the gatow, and it had a delicious taste of dark earth.

I don't have many magic bottles, so I don't make gatow too often. Only on special occasions, like when I defeat a powerful enemy or when I celebrate victory with friends. I don't understand how the bottles work, but I don't need to understand to make magical gatow.

CRUSHED STUFF PANCAKE

I have an easy and tasty recipe, orc-style. Find a cave or dungeon with a dead-end. Run in screaming to scare the creatures and monsters, and they will come into the dead-end. Then block the dead-end, trapping the monsters, and jump on them repeatedly to flatten them into a nice pancake. Watch out for their sharp teeth and claws, as they can be painful.

Afterwards, let the pancakes dry and dehydrate. It takes time, but it's worth it. Cut circles out of the pancakes with a large knife, then stack the circles together. Drizzle honey or another syrup on top, it's important for them to stick together. I prefer honey, but you can use your preferred syrup.

Now it's ready. Enjoy your dried monster pancake with honey. It will keep you nourished throughout the day. I eat this all the time. It gives me strength and endurance for hunting and fighting.

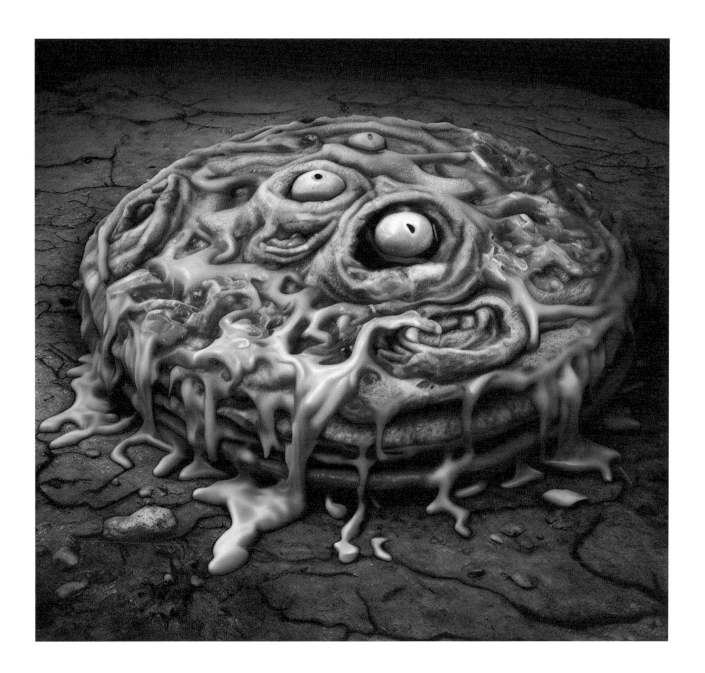

DWARF MUSHROOM FEET

Do you want a recipe for dwarf mushroom feet? I can help! To make a delicious and tasty dish, you will need fresh dwarf feet, a handful of poisonous mushrooms, and a jar of troll grease.

First, clean the dwarf feet and gently remove the nails. Place the dwarf feet in a large pot and add enough water to cover them. Bring to a boil and let simmer for 2 to 3 hours, making sure the feet stay submerged.

While the dwarf feet are cooking, heat the poisonous mushrooms in a skillet with troll grease until they are golden brown.

When the dwarf feet are tender, remove them from the water and place them in a serving dish. Arrange the poisonous mushrooms on top of the dwarf feet and generously pour melted troll grease over them.

Serve the hot dwarf feet with a cold dark beer for a truly satisfying meal!

MICE CRUSTY BREAD

To make this recipe, you will need several mice. First, find leaves and fruits and place them in a corner of a cave. Pour a mixture of troll fat and honey over them to make it very sticky. Wait a few days.

Return to the cave, and you will find several mice stuck to the mixture. Use a knife to peel off the vegetation and mouse crust, then roll it into a mouse crusty bread. You may need to press firmly to make the crust hold together.

You can now enjoy the mice crusty bread. I like this recipe because it uses natural ingredients from the cave. Mice have a good taste, but they can be difficult to catch. If you're lucky, you can catch several mice to make more mice crusty bread.

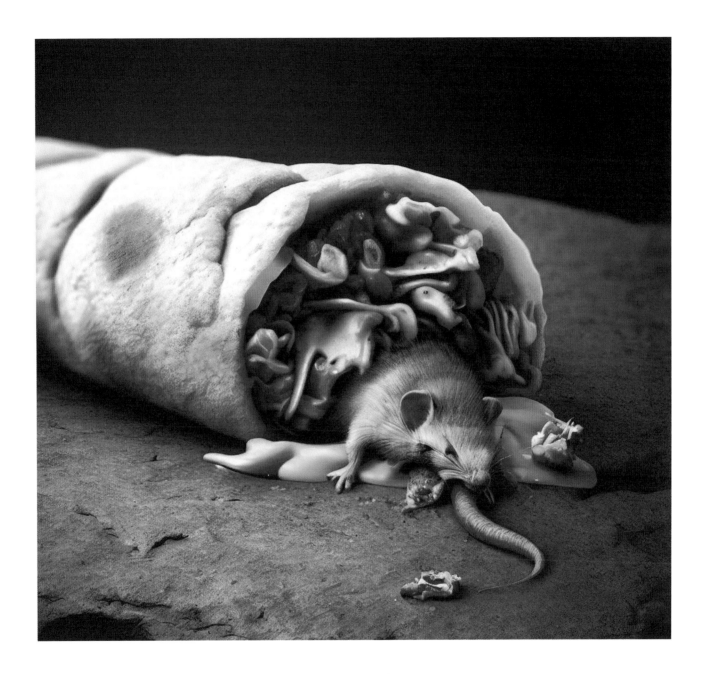

FINGER HOT DOG

I learned this recipe after a great battle. No waste, everything can be eaten, even the fingers of your opponents! Listen to me, you cut off the fingers and boil them for a long time. If they have nails, you can remove them, but I prefer to keep them for a bit of crunchiness.

Then, you make long buns, cut open the bread and put the fingers inside. Add sauce according to your taste. I like a bitter sauce with fire ash and hair grease. It gives a delicious and strong flavor.

This recipe is the favorite meal of orc children. They enjoy playing with the fingers before eating them. You might think it's disgusting, but for us orcs, it's normal.

GREEN BLOB WITH COARSE SALT

When I explore deep caves, I often encounter groups of dangerous green blobs. They have skin that burns, so you shouldn't touch them with your hands! But I am brave, so I try to catch them with thick bags. They can't do anything when they're inside the big bags.

I had a lot of trouble figuring out how to eat the green blobs, but I found a way! Just sprinkle a lot, lot, lot of coarse salt on them. The green blobs don't like salt and become paralyzed. After eating a green blob, the salt masks its taste. It's like eating just salt. so I figured out how to eat the green blob!

I enjoy eating the green blob. It's like an enemy. I like eating enemies.

45

FRIED GOBLIN HEAD

I have a recipe to get rid of goblins. These annoying little creatures always bother orcs; goblins are like rats, they're everywhere. But with this recipe, you won't have any more problems with goblins!

First, you catch the goblins, which is easy since they're always in large, noisy groups. Catch them one by one and put them in a big pot. Boil a large pot of oil and put plenty of goblin heads in it. I won't say how long, you just need to watch the color of the goblins' eyes. When their eyes turn red and explode, it's ready!

If you're a true warrior, you eat them with your hands. Consume them immediately to feel the burning sensation in your mouth. If you're not a warrior, you can use utensils. I prefer eating with my hands, as it adds a bit of spiciness.

HONEY HELMET

I have a recipe with an old adventurer's helmet. You don't need to be a genius to make this recipe, it's very simple.

First, you need to find a beehive. Beehives are easy to find because bees fly everywhere in the forest. Once you've found the beehive, take it and crush it quickly inside the helmet so that the bees don't have time to escape from the hive.

All the bees will die in the honey, but you shouldn't waste the honey. Take a handful of honey and bees directly into the helmet. Yum yum, it makes a delicious mix! You can also make this recipe with a wasp nest.

Be careful, as the bee venom will numb your mouth a little. So, you should be prepared for that strange sensation in your mouth.

MAGMA POKE BOWL

For this recipe, you'll need a large, thick stone bowl. Not a wooden or metal bowl, just a stone bowl.

The first thing you do is go to a cave near a magma river. Be careful not to get burned, as magma is very hot. Dip the stone bowl into the magma to fill it. If the bowl isn't big enough, use multiple bowls.

Next, take raw monster meat. Not rabbit or chicken meat, no, monster meat. Cut the meat into pieces, but not too small. You want to taste the meat, not eat it in one bite.

Put the raw monster meat into the magma-filled stone bowl. But not just the meat, also add seaweed, mushrooms, rock moss, and earthworms. Don't mix them, just place everything on the surface of the magma.

The magma will cook everything on its own. Just wait until everything is cooked. But be careful, don't wait too long. If you don't eat the bowl quickly, the magma will turn into hard rock, and you won't be able to eat it. So, discard the bowl.

GIANT CENTIPEDE KALE

You need to find a giant centipede for this recipe. Giant centipedes are often hidden in the depths of caves. But be careful, the mother centipede is really big and dangerous. Don't make any noise and take a baby centipede.

Next, find some kale salad. Not easy to find, but it's often near human villages. Humans like to eat it. But you don't eat the kale salad, it's just for decoration. Kale is super disgusting, it's just for decoration.

Place the giant centipede on a bed of kale. To eat, take the giant centipede and take a bite. The juice is really good, you'll like it. But be careful, the giant centipede has legs and pincers, so you need to be prepared to avoid them.

And there you have it, a really good meal. Giant centipedes can be a bit difficult to find, but it's worth it. And the kale salad is just there for decoration. Don't eat it, as kale is super disgusting. It's important to remember that.

FISH HERBAL INFUSION

I have a recipe for you if you're thirsty. Take a large bowl and go to a river to collect water. Also, catch a fish and put it in the bowl. But not just the fish, also add a handful of riverbed sediment. It gives it a better taste. Then, leave the bowl out in the sun for many days. The fish will die and create foam, turning the water green. When it starts to smell bad, it's ready.

Now, you need to drink the liquid. Use a straw to drink it. But be careful, pay attention to the smell. The water tastes better if you smell it at the same time. And don't throw away the fish. Eat the fish as well. It provides more protein.

However, you don't have to use just fish. You can replace the fish with crab, oyster, or octopus. It will give a different taste. Try it with various seafood options and find your preferred choice. You'll have a dead fish and stinky water. But you'll enjoy it. You'll taste the essence of nature in your mouth.

BEHOLDER CHEESECAKE

I have a truly special recipe for brave guests. You'll need the eye of a beholder, a super dangerous magical creature. I survived a battle against one, so I have a magical eye at home.

For this recipe, you'll need a stone bowl, one cup of flour, one cup of sugar, one cup of milk, cheese, and a tablespoon of yeast. Mix all the ingredients together, then add the beholder eye in the middle. Don't forget to wear gloves, or you might be cursed with dark magic.

Next, bake the mixture in a hot oven for 30 minutes. When the cake is ready, take it out of the oven and carefully observe the beholder eye. Sometimes the eye moves on its own, but that's normal—it's the magic at work.

Once the cake has cooled down, cut a slice and serve it to your guests. Be cautious, as sometimes the beholder eye turns red and emits a disintegration beam. Make sure to warn your guests before serving the cake. If you fail to do so, your guests might perish, and you'll become a very lonely orc.

STINKY INSECT BREAD

Me orc, me like to eat bread with flies inside, you like too? Here's a recipe to make super gross bread. First, prepare dough with sugar, flour, yeast, and eggs; knead the dough vigorously. Then, take a large bowl and put the dough inside.

Place the bowl in the corner of the cave where you poop. Wait for a day, flies and other insects will stick to the dough. The dough is now super smelly, but that's what's good about it.

Next, take the bowl and put it in a super hot oven. Wait for a long time until the dough rises. It can take several hours. When the stinky smell spreads throughout the cave, remove the bowl. Flip the bowl to take out the bread.

Warning, eating too much of this can cause illness and you may die.

59

SEAFOOD SALAD

I have a strange and dangerous breakfast recipe for you, but are you ready to taste it? If so, I will tell you how to make it.

First, you go to the sea, but don't go too far because the sea is filled with big monsters that want to eat you. Stay at the shore and use a large net to catch a bunch of funny live fish. If you're brave, you can also dive into the water to gather seaweed, but be careful not to get attacked by the monsters.

Next, put the seaweed and funny fish in a big, not-so-clean bowl. The bowl should be dirty to give it a good flavor. Add homemade dressing, fish juice, or any other smelly liquid. The smellier, the better! Mix it well until the fish stop moving. That's a sign that everything is ready.

Now, you're ready to taste it. Sometimes the fish make you vomit, but it's okay; it's still good!

PICKLE AND BLOB BEER

You'll need a large barrel to let a bunch of pickles rot. Put the pickles in it, along with water and honey, and let it sit for a long time until it smells really bad.

Now, you'll have to venture into the dungeons to find a not-too-big blob monster. Big blobs are dangerous. Fight the blob with weapons until it's dead. Then, crush the blob into the barrel and mix it all together.

Let the barrel sit for a few more days to allow the beer to form. Before serving, add pickles to the beer for a quirky presentation. The pickles will float on the stinky beer.

You can drink a lot of this beer, but be careful! Pickle and blob beer can cause a lot of gas and may lead to flatulence for you and your guests. However, many will find it amusing because the gas can be quite entertaining.

BEAR-OWL EGG

First, you must find a bear-owl. It's a very dangerous animal that often attacks orcs to eat our babies. But we are smarter than them. When the bear-owl arrives, you run into the forest to find its nest. Look for eggs and steal as many as you can. Break the ones you can't take. The bear-owl won't be happy, but we are stronger than it.

Next, place the egg directly into a big fire. Don't cook it for too long, or the egg will become hard. Break the shell with an axe and eat the liquid inside. Bear-owl eggs are very nutritious and provide a lot of strength and courage.

If you succeed in eating this egg, you'll be considered a true orc warrior and respected by all. But be cautious, the bear-owl may still seek revenge. You must be ready to fight again if necessary.

ZOMBIE PORK WITH MUSHROOMS

I stumbled upon this disgustingly unique recipe by accident. One day, I found myself trapped in an old crypt, incredibly hungry, and ended up eating a zombie. I'm not sure why I ate that meat, but my stomach felt surprisingly satisfied afterward. The meat was incredibly tender and juicy, as if the zombie had marinated in a special sauce.

That's when I had a brilliant idea. I invented a recipe for zombie meat. You don't have to wait for a zombie to come to you; instead, you take a pig and tie it up in an old crypt. Leave the pig there for a few days, and when you return, the pig will have transformed into a zombie!

Be cautious; you don't want to get bitten by a zombie pig, or you'll turn into a zombie and won't be able to enjoy this delicious meat. You need to be very careful.

Next, bring the zombie pig back home. Build a large fire and roast the zombie pig over it. Add some mushrooms on top to give it some flavor. Yum yum, it's better than regular live pig!

SNOT BREAD

To make the bread, you'll need flour, honey, yeast, and an egg. Mix them all together to form dough balls. Let the dough rise a bit and then cook it over a fire.

It's gross and flavorless, but I have a trick to make it better. Take a handful of pepper and go bother a big troll or ogre. They'll be angry about being disturbed, but quickly throw the pepper in their faces.

When the troll or ogre sneezes a lot, place a tray of bread in front of them. Wait for the bread to get nicely coated with their snot, and then make a quick getaway.

I know it sounds disgusting, but that's what makes it good! Troll or ogre snot adds a unique flavor to the bread. You'll taste the essence of decay and foulness, but strangely, you'll want more.

GHOST SOUP

I stumbled upon an old kitchen in an abandoned witch's house. I took all the kitchen tools and burned down the house. I destroyed the ghost's home and trapped it in an old cauldron. I was very scared when I saw the ghost in the cauldron! It made a lot of noise, so I poured boiling water over it. It turned into a liquid and stopped making noise, and that's when I got the idea to create a recipe for ghost soup.

I understand that you might be hesitant to use a ghost in cooking, but I promise it's delicious. You'll taste the essence of death and magic in the soup. You'll feel the presence of the ghost in every bite.

I've made this recipe several times now, and I always find it delicious. Holy water makes the soup gooey, but it's even better that way. You'll feel the magic of the soup flowing into your stomach.

ONION PLATTER

Do you want to impress your guests with a delicious appetizer? Just serve onions! Yes, you heard that right, just onions.

I know that everyone loves onions, so I have the perfect recipe for you. Slice the onions and boil them in water. Roast them over a fire until they're golden and crispy. Let them rot under the sun to add a touch of flavor. Dry them and mix them with spices to make onion powder.

But do you know what's even better than cooked onions? Raw onions! Chop them into small pieces and serve them with a vinegar and salt-based sauce. Everyone will say "wow" when you present the onion platter.

And you know what? Onions taste good in your mouth too! You'll have the smell of onions in your mouth all day. It's the perfect recipe to impress your guests and make them feel like strong orcs.

SPIDER STEW

Are you in a hurry to head to battle? I have a simple recipe for you, busy orc. Just place the ingredients in a large pot and let it simmer slowly over a small fire or next to the magma all day. It will be ready when you return.

I always like to simmer a lot of giant spiders. They become dry and crispy in the black venom broth. If you have a strong stomach, you can eat the entire pot without dying.

I start by crushing giant spiders and putting them in the pot. Add salted water until it covers everything. Then, place hot stones in the pot to help with the cooking.

Let it simmer all day. Sometimes I add pieces of meat, but only if I've killed an animal in the morning. Otherwise, the giant spiders are the sole source of protein.

ABOUT GRÛSH

Grûsh the Disgusting is a renowned orc chef in the world of orcs and goblins, celebrated for his original and bizarre recipes. His career began in the depths of dungeons, where he started cooking unusual ingredients such as giant centipedes, spiders, and even beholders.

His culinary talent quickly became known to other orcs and started spreading through the dungeons and underground caverns. Grûsh honed his craft by experimenting with new ingredients from other races, including trolls, ogres, and even humans.

Over time, Grûsh became a respected chef in the orc world, receiving invitations to cook at banquets hosted by the most influential warlords and goblin lords.

Today, Grûsh is considered one of the greatest orc chefs of all time. His fame extends far beyond the underground caverns and is even known in the realms of humans and elves, although most of them refuse to taste his strange and eerie dishes.

Printed in Great Britain
by Amazon

34715854R00048